DINOTOPIA

DINOTOPIA

A Land Apart from Time

Written and Illustrated by James Gurney

TURNER PUBLISHING, INC.

Atlanta

TO DAN AND FRANKLIN, WHO HAVE BEEN THERE AND BACK.

I would like to thank the following people:
Betty Ballantine, Michael Brett-Surman, Linda Deck, Ralph Chapman,
my brother Daniel M. Gurney, and my wife Jeanette, with a special thanks to
Ian Ballantine and David Usher.

DINOTOPIA
A Land Apart from Time
Written and Illustrated by James Gurney

Published by Turner Publishing, Inc.
A Subsidiary of Turner Broadcasting System, Inc.
One CNN Center, Box 105366
Atlanta, Georgia 30348-5366

Produced by THE GREENWICH WORKSHOP
© 1992 James Gurney, Licensed by The Greenwich Workshop.

Library of Congress Catalogue Number: 92-080108
ISBN 1-878685-23-6
First Edition

92 93 94 10 9 8 7 6 5 4 3 2

Distributed by Andrews and McMeel
A Universal Press Syndicate Company
4900 Main Street
Kansas City, Missouri 64112

Printed in Italy by Amilcare Pizzi, S.P.A.

PREFACE

A CENTURY AND A HALF AGO, Sir Richard Owen coined the word *Dinosauria* to name what he believed to be "fearfully great lizards." During the time since then, the earth has coughed up new bones faster than paleontologists can raise them up in marble halls. As we crane our necks upward, young and old, trying to reclothe those bones with muscle and skin in a kind of reverse X-ray vision, we keep asking ourselves: what were they really like?

We have moved into this earthly abode without the benefit of meeting the previous tenants. In this instance, the previous tenants had a lease of 150 million years. They must have gotten along well with the landlord.

The book you hold in your hands is an odyssey for the eye. You can check with the nearest eight-year-old; all the dinosaurs are real, based on fossil evidence. Whether the rest is real depends on you. It belongs in the marble hall, not of the museum, but of your imagination, the other side of the mirror, the world that is in the end more true.

Windy Point

Crystal Caverns •

SHIPWRECK **X**
The Hatchery •

Baz •••

Pooktook •

Volcaneum •

Polongo River

Temple Ruins •••

NORTHERN PLAINS

CRACKSHELL POINT

Cornucopia •
Deep Lake

Treetown •
• Bent Root

BACKBONE MOUNTAINS

)(*Rocky Pass*

Prosperine •

Sapphire Bay

• Poseidos
(sunken)

Hadro Swamp

R A I N Y

B A S I N

Waterfall City •

GREAT CANAL

FORBIDDEN MOUNTAINS

Amu River

SKY GALLEY CAVES •

Tentpole of the Sky

Sky City •

Thermala •

Canyon City •
• Pteros

Ancient Gorge

Warmwater Bay

Culebra •

OUTER ISLAND

Sculpted Cliffs •••

Red Rapid
Canyon
The Sentinels

••• The Time Towers

★ Sauropolis

GREAT DESERT

The Portal

Dolphin Bay

Dragonfly Coast

BLACKWOOD

FLATS

• Chandara

DINOTOPIA

KILOMETERS 0   25   50   75   100

STATUTE MILES 0   25   50   75   100

Cape Turtletail

[7]

HOW I DISCOVERED
THE SKETCHBOOK

NEARLY A YEAR has gone by since I first made the discovery. It was purely by chance. I was tracking down some information about the spice trade in China when my eye fell upon a curious old leather-bound sketchbook. The University library has hundreds of original manuscripts like it. They have all been catalogued, but few have been studied in detail.

At first it seemed to be just another sketchbook diary of a forgotten explorer. All the names were unfamiliar to me:

DINOTOPIA, by Arthur and William Denison, Being the Account of our Adventures and Discoveries on a Lost Island.

I quickly paged through it, for the librarian had rung the closing bell, and I had to get home. The book had been badly worn and water-damaged long ago. A very old photograph of a man and a boy slipped from its mount. Pressed into the back pages were some brittle botanical specimens of horsetail ferns and ginkgo leaves.

The drawings showed people and dinosaurs living side by side. But this was an impossibility. Dinosaurs had disappeared from the earth nearly 65 million years ago, long before mankind evolved.

Was this sketchbook a mere fantasy, or had I stumbled upon the only surviving record of a lost civilization? Honestly I have my own doubts, being skeptical by nature. But I offer you the facts of the case so you can form your own conclusions.

James Gurney

Will and Arthur Denison

Journal of Arthur Denison

November 10, 1862

HAVING LOST all my shipboard journals in the disaster of nine days ago, I will begin with the wreck itself, and the curious events that have followed.

Alas, our schooner *Venturer* has perished, along with all hands, save only my son Will and myself. We had been two years at sea, departing Boston on a voyage of discovery, through which I hoped to distract my son from the recent loss of his mother, and to assuage, somehow, my own grief.

We were sailing in uncharted waters when a typhoon struck with sudden fury. It ripped loose the topsail and brought a spar down, shrouds and all, with a glancing blow to my shoulder that left me nearly senseless. I do recall Will's pulling me loose before the foaming surge carried us both into the mountainous waves, and I can still feel the sensation of being lifted bodily to the surface by a dolphin, no doubt one of the same that had been following our vessel since we left Hong Kong.

With the last of our strength, we clung to the fins of the dolphins, who carried us into calmer green seas. We reached a line of breakers and soon our own feet could carry us to shore — blessed shore! — where daylight woke us, parched and groggy.

A strange
sign of life

By morning my shoulder, though stiff, was usable, and Will proved wholly uninjured. We searched the shoreline for a sign of the ship or our companions, sadly, in vain. But we did find, to our delight, a freshwater stream to answer our raging thirst. The dolphins followed our movements from a few hundred yards seaward, leaping and chattering, from all appearances trying to get our attention. In any case, I waved back, and Will hallooed as well, with the hope of reassuring and thanking them for our deliverance.

All at once Will put a hand to my shoulder and hissed, "Father, listen!"

From some distance in the jungle came a series of low, sustained hootings — or perhaps I should say bellowings — and then again silence. We waited. All remained quiet. Eventually, urged forward by our need to escape the hot sun, we crept into the jungle. Two reluctant Crusoes, we set about to make camp, clearing a stand of small tree ferns and looking for any fruit, berries, or game animals that might provide sustenance — an activity Will tackled with enthusiasm.

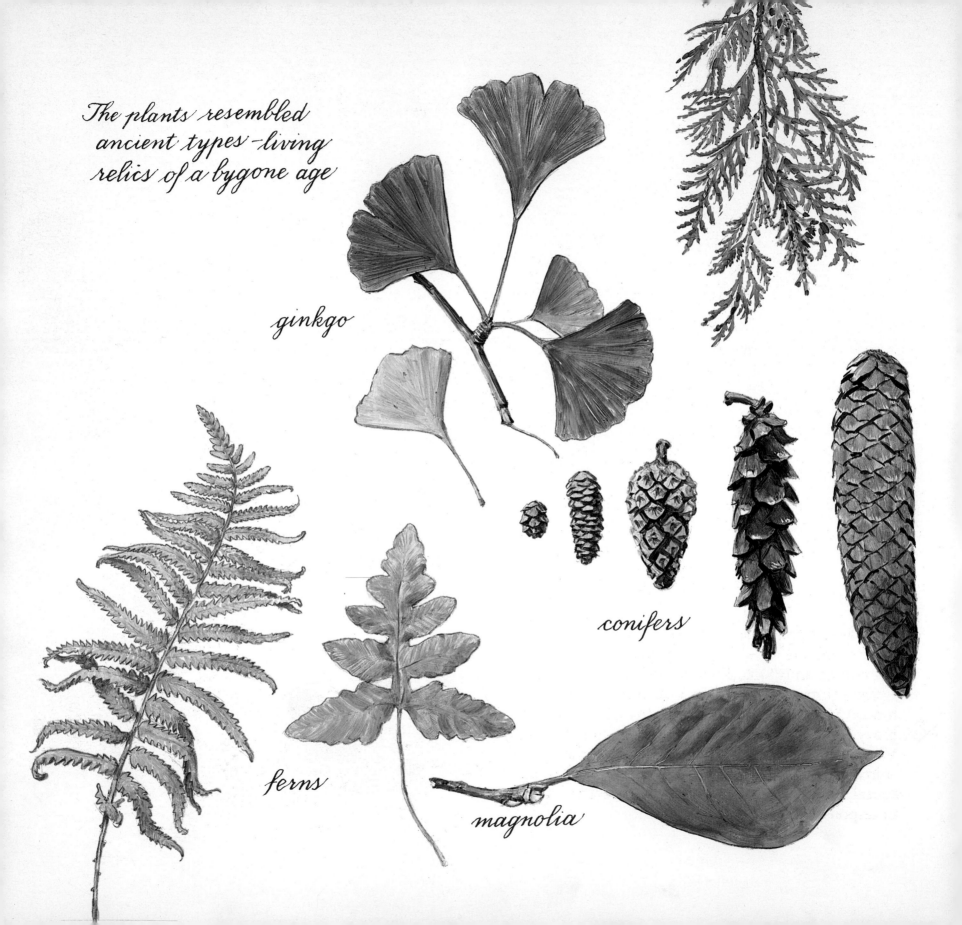

*The plants resembled
ancient types – living
relics of a bygone age*

ginkgo

conifers

ferns

magnolia

The creature was not seriously hurt

I was just preparing a brave speech for my son when a creature appeared — hog sized but somewhat resembling an iguana. It circled us, squawking like a parrot through its beaklike mouth, reaching a foot toward Will as though seeking a meal. I seized a heavy rock and waited for it to come within range. Whereupon I hurled the weapon, striking the animal on the leg. It let out a loud, anguished squeal. Instantly the bellowing began again, as if in response, and now much closer.

[15]

Within seconds the jungle erupted with a horde of creatures so extraordinary that I was immobilized, incredulous. Not so Will. He seized me and started to drag me toward the water. Too late!

Moving with terrific speed despite their size, the creatures surrounded us, displaying an armament of horns and club-like tails. Their stamping and bellowing deafened us. I realized that we were being threatened — and I hesitate even now to set this down — by *living* members of the class of vertebrates known as *Dinosauria*!

I had just thrust Will behind me, preparing to do I know not what, when to my utter amazement, a young girl emerged from behind the largest creature and soothed it with whistles, cooing noises, and gestures. She then approached the injured hog-parrot and made a bandage from her white head-dress. I was dumbfounded — and a little embarrassed. I turned to reassure Will, who was gazing awestruck at the girl.

At last the hog-parrot, which had been watching us intently, squawked out sounds something like "*Ank — ayyank-leesh. Yank-ank-kee.*" There followed a lively exchange of hoots, rumbles, head-bobbing, and foot-stomping, until, of a sudden, the hog-parrot was lifted on to the back of another of its kind, and the entire menagerie disbanded: judge, jury, lawyer, and clerk, leaving us alone with a club-tailed bailiff and the girl herself, who beckoned us to follow.

She spoke in a reproachful tone to us, using a language in which I seemed occasionally to hear a familiar word. So I made a couple of efforts: "*Pardonnez-moi, m'amselle?*; Er — *Entschuldigung?* Do you speak English?" To no avail, although she cocked her head as though she understood a word or two. However, her main concern was for the injured animal, which seemed to be making a great fuss about a minor hurt. Meanwhile, I kept a wary eye on the larger creatures, who maintained a constant rumbling and shifting about us. I urged Will to keep very still.

Reassuring a Triceratops

Both Will and I were tired, not only from our watery ordeal, but also from the shock just suffered. Nevertheless, Will set out sturdily, and even turned to offer me assistance! His two years at sea have made him more than usually rugged and self-reliant for a twelve-year-old. Together we trudged in the wake of the young girl for what must have been two hours, without any further attempt at conversation.

Wearily we walked behind her as the jungle gave way to pastureland. The road was twice the breadth of those in America. In the muddy places I measured wheel ruts fifteen feet apart, accompanied by hoofprints, not of horses or oxen, but of three, four, and five-toed giants. The girl and her escort led us to the heart of a large ranch, where we could see, coming and going from high stone doorways, more of the dinosaurs, including several of the family *Iguanodontidae*, with whom I was already well acquainted. To my astonishment, these creatures — which so recently had threatened us — were allowed to roam free of fences or harnesses, strutting about like roosters in a farmyard, and accorded the greatest respect by all of the people.

At the ranch the girl introduced herself, with signs, as Sylvia, a reassuringly familiar name. Her parents are Giorgio and Maria Romano. Kind souls, they are workers in what turns out to be a dinosaur hatchery, and, I must say, somewhat henlike in their manner. Maria clucked and patted Will, while Giorgio, with immense care, arranged a nest-like bed for our comfort. By early afternoon (as far as I could judge with my pocket watch rendered useless by the saltwater), we had eaten, bathed, and retired gratefully to bed.

The Egg Hatchery

Creatures the size
of ostriches care
for the eggs,
keeping them
warm in transit.

The guest bed was made
in the form of a nest.

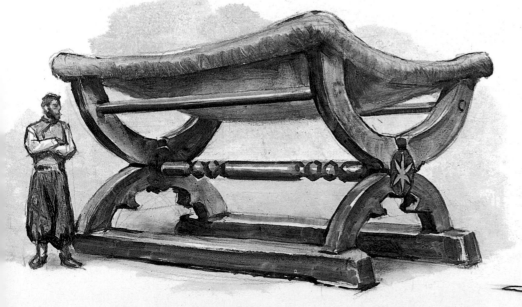

A dinosaur "chair" — or more
accurately, "resting-couch,"
since the larger quadrupeds
do not sit.

I now know how a chick feels, hatching into the expectant gaze of its companions in the henhouse. Giorgio must have been sitting beside us for much of the eighteen hours we slept. Maria, meantime, had washed my clothes free of salt and restored them to me. She then offered Will some pantaloons and a shirt of local origin, handwoven and of good substance.

At breakfast, to our keen delight, we were introduced to a gentleman named Alec Orchardwine, who spoke an archaic form of English. He seemed to search the air above his head for words, then said to Will something that sounded like *Wilcome, wee laddie.* He then pointed to a painting of a dolphin as if he knew the means of our rescue. He referred to himself as "fifteen mothers English," by which I was to understand that his ancestors had landed here fifteen generations ago, or some 400 years. There may have been some error of language here.

From this gentleman I learned that we are on an island named Dinotopia, that all humans here are descended from shipwrecked men and women, brought to safety by the dolphins, and, most astonishing of all, that Dinotopia's main population consists of all manner of dinosaurs, most of them peaceable, living as equals with the humans.

But if these harmless herbivores exist in such large numbers, what of the great carnivores? I cannot imagine a natural world more terrifying than one heavily populated by *Tyrannosaurus rex*. Will appears to be undismayed by our strange circumstances (the recuperative powers of the young never cease to amaze me) and was eager to explore the hatchery with Sylvia.

Breakfast was juice, tea, soup, bread, and nuts—no milk, no meat, and no eggs.

The Hatchery provides every comfort for expectant parents.

1. NESTING ROOM, with egg basins made of hardened clay, and a supply of ferns for padding.
2. PIPE ORGAN can be performed by large feet.
3. RESTING CHAMBER for conversation or relaxation.
4. INCUBATION ROOM, kept at about 101° Fahrenheit. Warmer temperatures will change developing embryos to males; cooler will result in more females. Basin of water over the fire keeps air humid, protecting the membrane inside the shell.

Sign at entrance of incubation room.

Waiting for the egg to be laid

5. HUMAN SLEEPING CHAMBER, with space for up to twelve full-time hatchery workers.
6. LIVING AND DINING AREAS for humans.
7. GUEST QUARTERS, usually occupied by humans traveling with expectant dinosaur females.
8. STAIRWAY to windmill for servicing gears and power assembly.
9. SIGNAL TOWER with faceted quartz stone.

In Dinotopia, most dinosaurs lay only two or three fertile eggs in their lifetime, a trait evolved in response to the scarcity of predators. In this way the population is stabilized. Laying an egg, then, is a major event in a dinosaur's life.

Ovinutrix (Egg Nurse) --known elsewhere as Oviraptor (Egg Stealer)

Albumen

Yolk Sac

Amniotic Sac

Embryo

Allantois

Inside a dinosaur egg, halfway through incubation

[27]

The children keep a close watch over the eggs.

Before hatching, the eggs squeak

Puppets help the babies imprint to the correct parent model.

Young Maiasauruses
enjoy being lifted
up to meet a
visiting aunt.

The children seem
marvelously
inventive and
co-operative in
their play.

Toys are fashioned
after a child's
favorite dinosaur

Lambeosaurocycle

Over-worked human parents
are fortunate to have
the help of
dinosaur nannies.

ball filled with
burdock flowers,
a dinosaur 'catnip.'

SOME DAYS have passed since my last entry. Happy news! My sea chest containing oilskin-wrapped sheets of foolscap and my notebooks was washed ashore amongst other wreckage. I will no longer have to borrow the precious paper of this household for my sketches and notes.

This land is a Mecca for a biologist. How Burton and Livingstone — indeed, Darwin himself — would envy the chance to document such a place, even if it meant, as I have just done today, playing nanny to a herd of young hadrosaurs.

Will and I continue to study the island's local language, apparently a blend of many, at which he is proving far more rapid a student than I. He spends much of his time with Sylvia, very much taken with the idea of a mere girl who can control such great creatures. He is eager to learn how to do so himself, even assisting Sylvia with her charges — all the youngsters who help at the hatchery. He accompanies her every afternoon on long walks to the seacoast in the vain hope of finding more wreckage or survivors. He may have missed the companionship of young people during our long sojourn at sea.

Our kind hosts have been pecking at me with eager questions about the outside world. I have told them a little about Darwin and Huxley's new theories and have described, to their infinite amusement, the recent display of life-size dinosaur models at the Crystal Palace in London. They seem relatively uninterested in developments like the compound steam engine.

My own inquiries are met with remarkable frankness, but I take little cheer in the latest revelation from both Giorgio and Alec that no one has ever left the island. As they say, "No eggs have rolled out of the nest." In their view, departure is synonymous with disaster because Dinotopia is surrounded by an impassible coral reef and a system of tides and winds that prevent navigation. I cannot believe there is no way of leaving and am determined to do so. Moreover, Will and I are expected to register our arrival at a place called Waterfall City, and to supply a list of our skills. This sounds too much like regimentation to me but I shall, for the time, cooperate. However, I must gain command of the language — a matter of several weeks, at least — before planning any further.

The time has come to move on. Giorgio has been watching the road for a vehicle to take us south along the coastal route, known as the Mudnest Trail. Sylvia and Will have borne the prospect of their parting better than I would have expected, though from their whisperings, I wonder if they have been working out plans to see each other again.

Barter has replaced coinage as a system of exchange.

Giorgio and Alec coping with an injured foot of a hard-working brachiosaur.

A dung wagon being readied for work. This vehicle, the only transport available for our journey, is certainly no Cinderella coach.

*The first evidence of civilization —
mysterious ruins of a lost city.*

We have been a day now on the road to Waterfall City, having won the blessing of the entire hatchery — human and dinosaur alike — to depart. Our transport, a dung wagon, is a more ill-smelling vehicle than any I have ever encountered in London, New York, or even Philadelphia. We are the only humans aboard. Besides the dinosaur in harness, there is a group of small reptilians who ignore us, despite Will's obvious interest in them. They are long in conversation in a language that sounds to me much like the squeaking of wheels. But I do hear time and again the word Pooktook, which I have understood to be a city of some size and sophistication that lies along our route.

Copro Carts are kept spotlessly clean.

On the outskirts of Pooktook, we were met by a crew who proceeded to fill our dung wagon with the noxious droppings of the dinosaurs. The material is rich in nitrogen, more resembling bird guano than horse manure. It will be carried to the surrounding farms to enrich the soil. Dinosaurs are remarkably efficient at processing their wastes. They do not urinate at all: their food is almost completely digested.

The men who collect the dung call themselves Copro Carters, and claim to be of noble lineage, bearing themselves with immense dignity, and a kind of slow thoughtfulness akin to those they serve. One fellow took Will and me for connoisseurs of fertilizer, recommending his exquisite age-ripened product as a Frenchman might speak of Gruyère or Camembert.

Simultaneously Will and I pleaded urgent business in the nearby city of Pooktook and left as rapidly as politeness allowed.

large cities often have conveniences

Method for descending stairs.

[37]

A Muttaburrasaurus with a message-rider. Each small Dimorphodon can memorize messages and will deliver them to various destinations— somewhat like a cross between a carrier pigeon and a parrot.

Human-powered taxi

The signs were written in a strange script

Traffic guide

Tuojiangosaurus

We have spent all day about the streets of the city, Will and I both agape. Side by side, the people and dinosaurs crowd the broad avenues, the street markets, the grand open-air theaters. I can only compare the spectacle to a Paris in which the doors of the zoological gardens have been thrown open and hippos lounge in the marble fountains of Versailles while sidewalk cafes cater to amiable rhinos. Yet at its outer fringes, Pooktook lacks much of this cosmopolitan flavor. In the gathering darkness, carpenters and wheelwrights, potters and tinsmiths were still at work, accompanied by much banter and laughter. Most of the houses were open to the evening air, exhaling breaths of curry and cider.

Will and I were debating the possibility of getting some food when a shadow detached itself from the nearby gloom and addressed us in rusty English: "Shipwrecked, are you? Lost? Needing a guide?" He tugged the brim of his hat over one eye and grinned. "Lee Crabb, if I may intrude myself. I'm a new starter here, too. Been nine years since a dolphin bucked me on to a beach."

We told him, rather guardedly, of the wreck of the *Venturer*, of our reception at the hatchery, and of our intended journey to Waterfall City. He listened with a sour grin.

"Dino-topia," he said slowly. "You think the name means a utopia of dinosaurs. Wrong. Look it up. It means 'terrible place'. I know. I've seen it. The skinnies are the slaves of the scalies. We're all slaves: hatching their eggs, hauling their dung. Or like me, I'm a slag man. Escape? Not today nor tomorrow. You've had your last grog and your last roast mutton, my good friends, my good skinnies."

Lee Crabb showed us his wagon, designed for carrying copper, bronze, and iron ingots. He is bound not for Waterfall City, but for the factory town of Volcaneum, which he recommends as a place to live and work without drawing attention.

He lifted his hat brim to peer down the now empty street. He then confided his extraordinary plan for escaping Dinotopia. Apparently it involves creating gunpowder from the dung with — he assumes — my 'scientific' help. It sounds absurd to me, and there is something in Mr. Crabb's manner that does not put me entirely at ease. But at the moment he is the only person who has echoed my own desire for returning home. Whether or not Dinotopia is the prison he claims, we shall see once we get to Volcaneum.

Lee Crabb

[43]

Because dinosaurs take pride
in their immense strength,
they do not look down on
"heavy work."

Crabb required my gold watch
in exchange for his services
as a guide.

'Gastrolith,' a
Pachycephalosaurus

[44]

A settlement near Volcaneum

The casting and forging room, overlooking
the caldera. Rutiodon helps with the bellows.

Tok Timbu

On reaching Volcaneum, Crabb set to work to earn some credits. His dome-headed companion, Gastrolith, turns one of the large wooden devices that operate the lathe room. It would seem that Crabb more often does the bidding of Gastrolith than vice versa.

When we first met the chief craftsman in metals, Tok Timbu, in the doubtful company of Crabb, the mastersmith fixed me with a gaze like a tiger. But he was impressed when I sketched, from memory, diagrams of the workings of foundries and mills I had observed back home. As we got to know one another, I believe he became convinced of my good intentions. Tok is a remarkable man, strong and a very talented artisan, with great personal dignity. He is "four mothers African," descended from a Yoruba king. Eventually I asked him about Crabb. Was he truly a slave, kept here against his will?

"Not at all!" Tok was emphatic. "No one leaves because no one can. Crabb has been trying for years. He finally gave up on finding the underground passage." Seeing my puzzlement, he went on, "There are old maps and old ballads — you'll see them in Waterfall City — that tell of caverns and tunnels underground. For a long time Crabb tried to find them." He shook his head and smiled. "We try to make him feel needed, but he'll probably never be at home here. Or anywhere else either."

Will and I live in a guest cottage but take most of our meals with the Timbu family. Their two sons are somewhat older than Will — a good influence. With my permission, Tok has put Will to work here, learning about the machines and tending the needs of the dinosaur-human teams. He is winning the respect of all. I wonder, though, how his mother would have regarded his new habit of bobbing his head and cooing like a dinosaur.

Door hinge and knocker made by Tok.

[48]

Arrival of a Skybax Rider

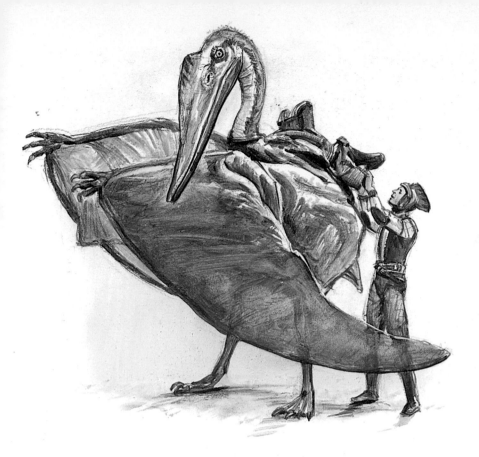

Tok told us that the saying has its origins with the dolphins, who long ago learned to survive by carrying deep drafts of air into the darkness of the waters. Dolphins owe their genial good nature and their playfulness to an almost perfect adaptation to their watery home, allowing them to flourish, despite being air-breathers. Or so says Tok. This greeting has found its way into many Dinotopian customs. For instance, the Dinotopian word for marriage or close friendship, *cumspiritik*, literally means breathing together. Sometimes land creatures hold out a claw or wing to represent the dolphin flipper — which has all the bones of the human hand. "Seek peace" comes from the dinosaurs, a reference shrouded in the mists of their history.

Some days ago the clouds above Volcaneum were pierced by a long, mournful cry. To my amazement, a leather-winged reptile swooped down, carrying a man on its back! As he landed a babble of greetings announced him to be a "Skybax Rider." He dismounted, unloading from his small saddlebag many treasures — maps, blueprints, medicines, and toys — while sharing the latest news from around the island. His mount is called a *Quetzalcoatlus skybax*, surely the most majestic flying creature the world has ever seen. None but the Rider himself dares to approach it, much less attempt to board it.

Will cannot conceal his fascination with flying. He lingers near the roost of the Skybax, and has adopted a new greeting, which he learned from the Skybax Rider. With a hand extended, he says: "Breathe deep, seek peace."

Ceratosaurus, a small cousin of Tyrannosaurus, but not as threatening

"Breathe deep, seek peace."

No fear of diving

walking using fingers

The Skybax Rider had just finished his work here, delivering new orders for the factory, when upon mounting his saddle, he turned to us with a simple remark that took us quite by surprise: "Will and Arthur Denison, they are waiting to welcome you at Waterfall City."

At which the Skybax spread its leathery wings and took to the clouds. Does the whole island know of our arrival? It is disturbing. Yet, on second thought, castaways are surely rare enough to create news of the first order. Meantime, Will has declared his determination to become a Skybax Rider!

[52]

Tok making jewelry for a Stegosaurus.

"A dolphinback like yourself learning to fly?" said Tok to Will. Newcomers are not expected to achieve such control of the wild creatures. But Tok has much confidence in the boy, and has laid before him the course for becoming a pilot: because he is a dolphinback he must first go to Waterfall City to learn writing, history, and ethics; then to Treetown, a summer camp where young people and dinosaurs practice living in accord; and finally to a canyon in the east where pilots win the trust of their reptilian partners. I expressed to Tok my doubts about Will's maturity. Tok eyed me and remarked, "Arthur, your son is reaching out for responsibility. You must learn to let him learn."

He is right. I am too anxious. Tok has been a tower of strength to my son, who has responded with a new sense of purpose. Meantime my own thoughts of an eventual return home have turned to the old maps Tok mentioned.

Going to Waterfall City might provide me with an opportunity to find out more about them.

Bix, a Protoceratops

I agreed with Tok's suggestion that we have a guide for our journey, but I was not prepared to see the hog-parrot again. Tok pointed out that the creature is female. To be precise, her name is Bix, of the species *Protoceratops multilinguous*, an ambassador and translator, one of the few dinosaurs who can 'speak' human languages. She remembered me, and said, "Breathe deep. Seek peace, Arthur Denison. No rocks, I hope?" Evidently she has a sense of humor.

male   *female*

[55]

Bix and Will
are fast friends

The capacity for gentle affection among
these creatures is astonishing. I now
understand Bix's exaggerated
reaction to the minor injury I
inflicted, unaccustomed as she is
to any deliberate attack.

She still sports a bandage — utterly
useless, but I believe she is
quite proud of it.

THE FOLLOWING DAY we started out, descending the volcano on its eastern flank, while before us the great valley of the Polongo River stretched out to a limitless horizon. The clear air, the amber sunshine, Will's eager interest in all things, and my private hope of discovering a means of escape enabled us to bear the difficulties of the road, which was frequently crossed by streams or scarred by deep wheel ruts. Had our legs been ten feet long, as were some of the giants Bix described, the fallen logs and muddy mires would have offered no obstacle. Nevertheless we kept steadily on, Bix commenting and explaining as we went. I learned, among other things, that she can understand seven-teen major languages, including Etruscan, Hittite, and Hypsilophodont, and can mimic, with absolute precision, the bubbling of a sulphur spring, and many other sounds in nature.

After several hours she announced, "Short cut," and led us away from the road at a point where it veered to the south. She might as well have said "Wet feet," for the route we now followed drew to the edge of a vast, shallow swamp.

She directed us to a thicket of totora reeds, nipped off a quantity with her beak, and showed us how to bind them into a serviceable boat, much like those used by the fishermen of Lake Chad. "Old Dinotopian design," she said.

Our boat brought us to a settlement of crested hadrosaurs and their human assistants, where we spent a few days drying out in the smoky attics of their houses.

Each of the hadrosaurs was equipped with its own distinctive resonating chamber, which it used to hoot at others of its own kind — even if those kinfolk were miles away through fog and forest. After a deafening concert of raspy honking, a hollow log was drummed to order silence, and all assembled craned their necks and stared into vacancy, listening for the answering foghorn.

The humans then took their turn with matching instruments and costumes. Those people waiting to perform shut their eyes and puffed out their cheeks like frogs who have swallowed fat flies. Such serious pomp and bombast I had not seen since a visit to the United States Senate.

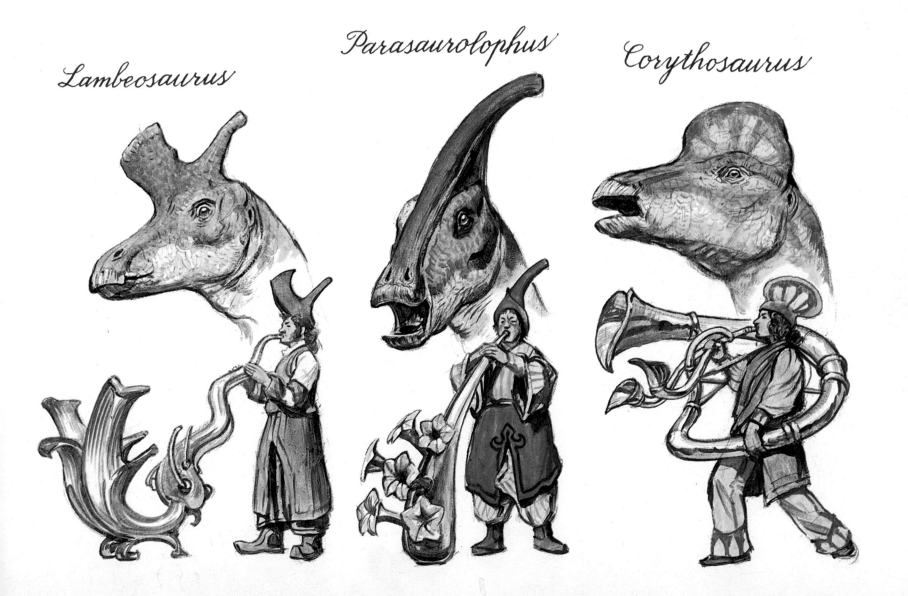

Lambeosaurus

Parasaurolophus

Corythosaurus

Hylaeosaurus

Polacanthus

Euplocephalus

We shoved off early next morning. The music of the hadrosaurs gradually gave way to the distant, deep, steady reverberation of a great waterfall.

Along the banks of the stream, armored dinosaurs wobbled into the sunny places, giving the appearance as they stood side by side of a gently heaving cobblestone street. At intervals a head would bob up to watch us, and a mouth would bark out a warning — a warning which Bix most often translated as "Black rocks, white water." The now rapidly moving current did indeed gather even more force as we swept around the last bend. We had a single glimpse of the city before the boat overturned in the shallows. Climbing up the rocks and gasping for air, we beheld Waterfall City for the first time.

A first glimpse
of the city

[61]

From our high perch we gazed down on the foaming waters, wondering how we might make a crossing. All at once several objects which at first I took to be Skybaxes appeared above the city. They approached, and to my utter amazement, I saw they were flying vessels, with sail-like wings, coasting through the air without flapping, and steering directly for a flat table-top of rock not far below us.

At the very moment they settled to the earth, the captain of the largest craft unstrapped himself, secured the wings from the buffeting drafts of air, and approached us, introducing himself as a Wing Ambassador. He invited us aboard. Will scrambled to his place enthusiastically, followed by Bix. But I took some time, seeking first to convince myself that the silk and bamboo structure was sound and that our weight would not overload the vessel. Then, filled with apprehension, I boarded, trusting my life to the skill of the captain, who dashed out over the boisterous falls with an alacrity born of necessity.

Our flight gave us a clear
vista of the city and its great
dome, on which I was able to observe,
despite the circumstances, a vast map of
the continents. But the map-makers are sadly
confused, the land masses being all linked together
in a jumble. We soon skittered to a stop in a lofty, open
square, Will hallooing in a shameless display of high spirits,
while I dismounted with as much dignity as my soggy condition
allowed. A colorful crowd led us away through the swirling vapors.

Seldom, I am sure, have strangers been given such a welcome. So hearty were the greetings that I had little time to notice the magnificence of all about us. Presently we were standing in a long marble corridor, with the registry before us, which was in fact a long scroll. I saw names from many other nations and epochs, some in unfamiliar scripts. The atmosphere of warm enthusiasm overcame all my doubts. I wrote "Arthur Denison, Professor of Sciences, and son, William, August 6, 1863." We dressed in soft yellow robes while our other clothes were put to dry, and proceeded into a banquet hall festooned with laurel garlands, with many small birds flitting about among a company of merrymakers.

I am quite content to leave the privations of the trail behind me for a time. We are to stay in a hostelry maintained by the city for its many visitors. Inside, the thickness of the stone walls mutes the thunder of the waters, but there is always a steady background drone to remind one of the sublime glory of the city's setting.

Will and I spent several days in carefree wanderings, but eventually Bix suggested we might like to begin our formal studies. She said she had made an appointment for me with a distinguished *Stenonychosaurus* named Malik, the timekeeper for all of Dinotopia. Malik would be willing to instruct me about time.

I met him in his museum of clocks and sundials, which I studied with great interest. He showed me his most beloved treasures, including the newest acquisition, obtained from a Skybax Rider: a gold watch engraved with the initials "A.D.", cleaned and in perfect condition.

Stairway to the Time Door

Malik, the timekeeper

The watch was, of course, my own, the very one I had used to pay Lee Crabb for our trip to Volcaneum. As to how the Skybax Rider had obtained it I could only guess. No matter. Malik had begun a kind of chatter, with Bix translating: "You of the West," Malik said, "think of time moving in a straight line, from past to present to future. Your eastern brothers regard time as a circle, returning endlessly in a cycle of decay and rebirth. Both ideas have a dimension of the truth. If you were to combine geometrically the movement of the circle with the movement of the line, what would you have?" He snapped his mouth shut and peered at me with an uncanny resemblance to my old schoolmaster.

"The spiral?" I ventured.

"Yes, yes. Or the helix. They are our models of the passage of time," he said.

"So time moves on, but history repeats itself."

"Precisely," he said, apparently with some satisfaction. "Won't you come with me and have a look at our helicoid geochronograph?"

A pocket watch

We passed through another door and entered a chamber inside the spherical dome. A creaking wooden device, powered by water, turned a gigantic stone pillar, and as it revolved, a mechanism climbed up the spiraling ledge, reading with its sensitive fingers a series of notches and carvings. At intervals, colored flags would rise, whistles would sound, or pebbles would drop down on brass bells.

"What hour is it?" I asked, reaching instinctively for my pocket watch.

Malik took a step back. "Time for *Kentrosaurus* to hatch. Time to plant the millet. Time for the magnolia buds to open. Professor Denison, I'm afraid you persist in thinking of time as numbers. You think of meaningless units of time — weeks, hours, minutes — based on what? Movements of faraway planets? Of what use to us is that? Why not pay attention to the precise 30-year life cycle of the bamboo *Guadua trinii* or the exactly repeated mitotic cycle of the paramecium? The whole earth has a heartbeat."

He paused, swung his tail from side to side, and squinted. "And some things happen too slowly for you to notice. If you sit quite still, you can hear the grinding down of mountains, the stretching upward of trees, the pushing forward of continents — indeed the wearing away of this very waterfall."

"Surely not!"

"Yes, indeed. Every hundred years or so, we must divert the Polongo River and rebuild the cliff beneath the city."

Malik reached his clawed hand for a small silver box and handed it to me. "You will soon become a Dinotopian. And when you do, you will measure your life in a different way. Then this will be useful."

I hinged open the lid and saw a pocket version of the great spiral clock.

Crystal beacons relay signals throughout the land

A common street game in
Waterfall City. A four-sided top
is marked "put, take, all, or nothing."
Contestants take turns,
adding or subtracting
colored stones.

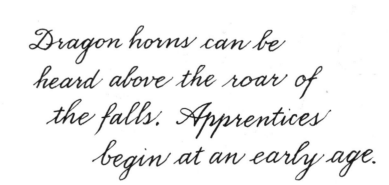

Dragon horns can be
heard above the roar of
the falls. Apprentices
begin at an early age.

Nallab

Bix then showed us to the library. A curious gentleman who called himself Nallab greeted us at the door. His eyes twinkled. "Learning to read?" he asked. "We use scrolls instead of books. Dinosaurs don't like to fumble with turning pages." A growl tore the air, and a *Deinonychus* craned his head to peer at us.

A Scroll-reading Machine in Operation

The footprint alphabet

Our host smiled. "This is Enit, our Chief Librarian," he said. "Perhaps he will show you his scroll-reading machine." Another growl and the machine rattled to life as Enit strained at the treadmill. Gears pulled the paper down past the viewing area and onto a reel in its base.

"Dinosaurs do their best thinking when their feet are moving," Nallab explained. "It comes from their ancestry. The early Dinotopian dinosaurs left footprint messages on stream banks — directions, warnings, poems, even jokes and riddles.

"If you were a young dinosaur," Nallab went on, twitching an eyebrow toward Will, "you'd learn to write in a sandbox. But instead we'll get you started with the quill of an *Osteodontornis orri*."

After his very active experiences at Volcaneum and the Hatchery, Will disliked the idea of being shut in with musty scrolls. But as he said to me privately, "I can stand any amount of studying as long as it will get me into a Skybax saddle eventually."

A B C D E F G H I
J K L M N O P Q R
S T U V W X Y Z ?
0 1 2 3 4 5 6 7 8 9

While Will started learning the Dinotopian alphabet, helped by Bix, Nallab escorted me on a tour of the library. From the outside, the building towers over the entire city; inside, the corridors and reading rooms are equipped with honeycomb shelves for the scrolls. In each room there is a fireplace. "Dratted mildew," Nallab grumbled. "A constant battle to keep the scrolls dry. A waterfall is a nasty place for a library."

He set to poking at logs while I scanned the shelves with eager eyes, forgetting what I'd come here to find.

By comparison to this vast storehouse of ideas, the Library of Alexandria would have seemed a puny collection cataloguing only the few short millennia of human wisdom. Dinosaurs have mused and argued and dreamed and reasoned for tens of millions of years, watching all things from their calm, wrinkled eyes.

I managed to translate just a few of the titles:

SONGS OF THE SEA TURTLES

HOW TO MAKE GOLD

PALEOZOIC POEMS

LESSONS FROM THE BEE DANCE

THE CARE AND TEACHING OF HUMANS

PERPETUAL MOTION MECHANICS

A COMPENDIUM OF HELPFUL FUNGI

MASTERPIECES OF TERMITE ENGINEERING

Stegosaurus

Chasmosaurus

Pachycephalosaurus

Ornithomimus

Saltasaurus

Actually, most Dinotopian writing is not even copied onto the scrolls. The hazy ideas, the gossip, the dull anecdotes, and the bad jokes are written out in a sandbox, where they can easily be erased. "The three-toed dinosaurs are always the scribes," explained Nallab. "They're fine dancers, with good clear footprints."

Northwest Pyramid

At Nallab's suggestion, I climbed the pyramid that loomed above the northwest corner of Waterfall City. Enshrined at the top was a tablet that translates as follows:

CODE OF DINOTOPIA

Survival of all or none.
One raindrop raises the sea.
Weapons are enemies even to their owners.

Give more, take less.
Others first, self last.
Observe, listen, and learn.
Do one thing at a time.

Sing every day.
Exercise imagination.
Eat to live, don't live to eat.
Don't p . . . (remaining text missing)

I heard a chuckle behind me as I finished sketching. It was Nallab. "You're probably wondering about that last line," he said. "The stone was broken when we discovered it, so we can only guess. I believe the last injunction applies only to humans: 'Don't pee in the bath'."

Nallab is a mine of information on matters Dinotopian. I even felt free to ask him about his age.

He cocked an eyebrow at me. "Well, now," he said, "how old do you think I am?" I guessed, cautiously, the early seventies. He cackled in high glee. "Shy by fifty years!"

"One-hundred-and-twenty?" I gasped.

"Actually one-twenty-seven. We are all very long-lived on Dinotopia — at least by your standards. Comes from that herb we eat —" he waved a vague hand.

I am incredulous of course, but did not hurt the good man's feelings by saying so.

Every day after the main meal, Nallab and I meet to explore a new corner of the city. We have wandered past canals and fountains, monuments and schools, gardens and observatories, kiosks and theaters — all woven into a watery labyrinth of stone that would shame even Venice.

"I can't imagine," I said one afternoon after a long silence, "how it could be possible for such a small island to support enough artists and stonecutters to build all these wonders. And I can't imagine how all these different people and dinosaurs can possibly get along without quarreling."

"Oh, it is possible," said Nallab, sucking thoughtfully on a mango, "but only if you *do* imagine it..."

February 8, 1864. Will and I have dropped anchor here in Waterfall City. We've been here six months now, and we discover new things every day. Perhaps we are enchanted by the mist, or we are beguiled by the siren song of the intellectual life. Nallab tells me that I will be expected to teach courses in Outer World sciences and developments. Between studies and teaching I doubt there will be much time for my notebook.

March 17, 1865. A year and a half in Dinotopia's center of learning. I have become something of a favorite at the library, and have spent much time correcting and updating the reports from previous shipwrecked sailors about the Outer World. The engineers study my diagrams with thoughtful respect, but they rarely carry my designs into action. The sewing machine, however, was met with enthusiastic acclaim.

A window to the dolphin caverns below the Aqua Stadium. Both Will and I have spent much time swimming, our chief form of physical recreation.

April 14, 1865. I have at last found the set of mildewed charts and old ballads mentioned by Tok. They are so primitive as to be useless. Indeed, Nallab says they are the basis of religious myths of a heavenly underworld sacred to dinosaurs, a curiosity rather than a practicality. Still, it's a puzzle I would like to have solved, even though I have lost any desire to leave Dinotopia.

The water slide is used by all, including small children riding the dolphins.

Whenever I grow weary from reading scrolls or exploring the vaulted passages below the city, I mount the high places in the western sector and sit beneath the Lion Statues where two long-toothed, ancient beasts, carved from red granite, crouch amid the thunder and mist. Bix told me the legend that at one time the falling water had no voice and was as silent as the clouds. But when the lions first arrived in Dinotopia, they were kept for a time on the bare rock that later became Waterfall City. Their roaring awoke the waters, provoking an eternal answering call.

Could there still be such lions alive on Dinotopia? I sometimes hear talk of the Forbidden Mountains, a colder region where a great variety of prehistoric mammals is said to thrive. Bix clarified. "Meat-eaters, yes," she said, "but not lions in the lowlands. *Tyrannosaurus rex*. When we set out to cross Rainy Basin we will have to be particularly careful."

And now the time has come. The thought of danger has preoccupied the lively family of ornithomimid scribes with whom we have been living since moving from the hostelry. They have been scurrying about, packing scrolls and ink in heavy wooden cases, and filling many cork-lined baskets with enormous quantities of strong-smelling smoked eel and shark-meat. I have absolutely no taste for either. They are preparing for their annual journey north to the Habitat Conference near Treetown. Will's studies are complete, and he and I are to accompany them. The route leads through the heart of danger, but it may be the only opportunity this year for us to make the trip to Treetown. He can hardly contain his excitement, though I shall be sorry to leave Waterfall City and the good friends we have made here.

Vertebral drawbridge.

SUCH PREPARATIONS! A full week was required. I spent two days simply fastening the stiff buckles joining the overlapping plates of armor for our *Apatosaurus*. Her name is Koro Kidinga. She bears her added burden with dignified resignation. By mid-morning of the day of our departure, sharp-spined *Styracosaurus* escorts had arrived. I protested to Bix that Will and I were neither warriors nor did we have weapons.

"Ours is an invitation," she said, "not a challenge. *Tyrannosaurus rex* is not evil. Only hungry by nature, with no love for society, and no stomach for green food. That is why we carry fish." I did not find this at all reassuring.

The convoy lurched into motion with a slow, rocking gait. We came to a drawbridge, the only crossing into the lawless jungle. The bridge had been engineered after the fashion of sauropod neck bones so that after we crossed over and Koro stepped off, the vertebral supports contracted and the bridge sprang back up like a pine branch relieved of a weight of snow. No retreat was possible.

The hundreds of pounds of fish and armor kept Koro to a deliberate shuffle. Long past midday, we moved through a grove of lofty *Lepidodendron* trees, heavily damaged by the gigantic strength of a troop of creatures that must have passed by recently.

Suddenly Koro lifted her head to the level of the treetops, fixed her gaze forward, and then wheeled around — with us clinging to our seats — so that her whip-like tail could sweep the perimeter of ground as an angry cat's tail will sweep the grass. At the same moment, snorting and bellowing, the *Styracosaurus* guards backed up into a circle around our unprotected quarter, presenting to the dark wall of jungle a fearsome row of horns.

Baskets of smoked eels

scribes

I can only compare her naive bravado to that of a squirrel whose nut has fallen to the feet of a passerby. Each time, a rising rumble or a clack of jaws was checked by a burst of scolding. Bix signaled to Will to start cutting loose the baskets. One by one they broke open with a thud as they hit the ground, while we edged away, leaving the creature to gorge.

I helped Bix back into the saddle. Will exclaimed, "Bix, what on earth did you *say?*"

"We made a deal," she replied, winking. "I told him he could have our snacks if he promised to leave alone the herd of defenseless prosauropods coming through tomorrow..." A deception which Bix modestly characterized as mere tact. I see why she is an ambassador! But it seemed to me a hazardous defense, at best, against a clear danger, no matter what Bix claims to the contrary.

With a heavy, bounding gait that shook the ground, a *Tyrannosaurus rex* broke into full sunlight. Close upon our circle it paused, eyeing us hungrily, opening its terrific jaws and clashing its teeth. Bix told Will to stand ready to cut free the baskets of fish while I tried to quiet the frantic scribes.

Then, to my horror, Bix leapt down from her perch in the saddle on to the back of a *Styracosaurus*, there to confront the attacker directly. Aghast, I watched as she addressed the creature by name, in a chattering discourse which seemed momentarily to confuse it.

*Ceratosaurus Gate
of the Temple Ruins*

For the next six days our exit from the Rainy Basin was confounded by a lack of trails and a series of difficult river crossings. The channels, it seems, are constantly changing. At last the caravan achieved its destination, a solemn ruin held firmly in the grip of the jungle at the base of the Backbone Mountains. Singly, or in groups, people arrived in the company of dinosaurs, who, having rid themselves of armor and baggage, ducked under the arch and entered the sacred space within.

'Brokehorn,' a Triceratops, addresses the assembly

Bix is well-known here.

Bix is well known here and was greeted by all with immense respect. That she has been designated as our personal guide makes me realize how important the dinosaurs consider the arrival of new humans into their society.

A dignified elder *Triceratops* with a broken horn rose to address the assembly that had now gathered. Will and I assisted the scribes, tending the sandbox of the footprint writers. Our time spent alongside the sandboxes in Waterfall City was not in vain, yet it did little to help us follow Brokehorn's quaint forest-hermit dialect.

He carved a high arc with his nose horn, wheezing. The scribes padded across the sand with great urgency. He then dropped his beak, lifted the frill, and barked. The scribes spun in circles. He swung his head to one side and hooted. The scribes trotted — and then paused.

Will elbowed me. "Father, they want *us* for something." I looked about. All eyes were upon us.

"Step forward," Bix whispered. "You have just been announced. We would like to make some introductions."

[87]

Lightwing and Oolu

Bracken and Fiddlehead

Bigtusk and Moraine

We met in turn each of the so-called Habitat Partners. Each pairing of human and dinosaur represents a different biological region. Together, their lifetime devotion is to monitor all living conditions within their territories, reporting annually at this conference. Based on the advice and help of the group, they would return home to supervise planting, pruning, and protection.

AERIAL: Oolu and Lightwing, a Skybax, responsible for watching weather, rainfall, pollen, dust.

FOREST: Bracken and Fiddlehead, a *Chasmosaurus*. An area of great responsibility, the renewal and health of woodlands and jungles.

ALPINE: Moraine and Bigtusk, one of the mammoths from the Forbidden Mountains. Their care: glaciers, tundra, high meadows, sulphur vents.

Dorso-lith and Seco

Paddlefoot and Magnolia

Draco and Highjump

DESERT: Dorsolith (a *Euplocephalus*) and Seco (five mothers Sonoran), masters of sand dunes, erosion, water management.

FRESHWATER: Magnolia and Paddlefoot, a *Lambeosaurus*, in charge of swamps, lakes, rivers.

SAVANNA: Draco and Highjump, a *Struthiomimus*, range open country to look after grasses, reeds, insects, soils.

BEACHES and BAYS: These are the charge of the dolphins who obviously could not be present. I was deeply impressed by the care and concern each sector displayed for the whole, and glad I'd had time to study Dinotopia's flora and fauna at Waterfall City. Will is in awe that he has actually been introduced to Oolu, the head Skybax trainer from Canyon City.

[89]

AFTER THE CONFERENCE ENDED, we continued north. All the way up the Backbone Mountains Will pestered Bix with questions about Canyon City. He had learned that her parents live near there, and in fact she was pleased to talk about her family. I kept quiet, saving my breath for the three-hour climb, but I, too, would like to meet her kin. We have grown very fond of Bix.

Eventually we drew near to Treetown. The village perches in the canopy of an oak forest, with a fine view of Deep Lake, and with tilled fields, barns, and botanical gardens within a short walk.

Bix departed for one of the barns to hear the latest gossip. We ascended ladders and were greeted warmly by Norah, matriarch of Treetown. She soon involved us in busy activity—supplies to be hoisted, yams to be washed, ropework to be mended—however, not before we had enjoyed a reviving snack of fried millet cakes in syrup, along with fruit and cold berry juice, followed by a rapid tour of the main trees. Norah climbs up and down the ladders without a thought, and to tell the truth I was only too glad to sit down to mending ropes.

A family of *Brachiosaurus* glided up from the valley below to receive their daily treats of fresh turnip ferns and water spangles. As the day wore on, Norah noticed how tired we were. She showed us our sleeping arrangements—Will in one of the boys' trees, I in the big central one—and fed us a bowl of soup while telling us of the late evening bell that signals all to rake up the fires, put out the lights, and retire. I was asleep before the bell rang.

Norah
of
Treetown,
3 mothers Irish

[91]

View of Treetown from my sleeping basket.
The lumber all came from a forest
leveled by a windstorm 300 years ago.

Sylvia of the Hatchery

I had scarcely pulled on my socks the first morning in Treetown when Will arrived, breathless and flushed with enthusiasm, to tell me that his friend Sylvia of the hatchery is among the girls staying here.

I am feeling my age. I have only surveyed the scene, but Will seems to be acquainted already with every twig, shingle, and slat of the village, as well as every inhabitant. Well, I will simply take my time about exploring.

The past several days have seen a wild change in Will. He met two boys from an eastern city called Chandara. They claimed to be expert rope swingers and dared him to take part in some dangerous stunts, unseen by Norah, who was busy about the larder. Then, after the curfew bell, when the boys and girls had retired to their separate sleeping quarters, he crept out of his basket, rallied with the boys from Chandara, and stealthily climbed into one of the girls' trees. With a fair imitation of a *Tyrannosaurus* growl and a few well-timed spins of the sleeping baskets, they set all the girls to screaming.

The following day, when Norah appeared, she cleared her throat and tapped on the balcony rail with a wooden spoon. I braced myself for a scolding. But she turned to Will, and said simply, "Young Mr. Denison, let us see that this does not happen again. May I ask that tonight you spend the night in the dinosaur barns. Try playing a *Tyrannosaurus* there. Now get to breakfast."

Once Will was out of hearing, Norah turned to me, sensing my embarrassment. "Don't worry about him, Mr. Denison," she said. "He's a lively boy and he'll grow up fine. But he needs to keep the company of dinosaurs."

Norah's granddaughter Melanie is visiting from Waterfall City. She listens to shells to remember the sound of the falls.

Will spent an uneasy night among the giants. He reported to me that he slept little, between the heavy shifting of feet, the wheezing and whistling noises, and the muffled crunch of rocks in their bellies (Bix has told us this helps them grind their food). At one point Will opened his eyes to see a great head, as large as a wheelbarrow, peering down from a few feet above him. The head swung up and vanished into the darkness of the rafters. His dreams were of walking trees, and mountains that could inhale and exhale.

As a result, Will's behavior has improved and he seems to be reapplying himself with vigor to his tasks. I have lately had many conversations with Sylvia, renewing our memories of the days at the hatchery. She has a sweetness of character, surely the clue to her extraordinary relationship to all dinosaurs. She and Will seem to be a good influence on each other. Their days are full with all they must do and learn, and so are mine. After I complete my daily chores for Norah, I explore this region and keep up the journal and field notes.

There is a wholly different class of flora at these heights. We must be at about 5,200 feet of elevation (or, as they prefer to say, 130 *necks*, each neck being a unit of approximately 40 feet). I have so far recognized great trees of rhododendron, an enormous variety of delicate ferns, tiny rock violets, and many tuberous wild lilies. Cool nights. Hot, sunny days. A paradise.

Brachiosaurs sleep in barns for protection from occasional stray carnosaurs.

One morning, Norah cheerfully said to me, "Arthur, it's time you had some company on your rambles. Take Melanie and Kalyptra with you." Melanie is her five-year-old granddaughter, and 'Kal' the *Dryosaurus* who always accompanies her.

Melanie

As we toured through thickets and brambles, Melanie would stop at a single tiny shoot in the midst of a mass of vegetation, and say, "My, how you've grown!" No bud or tendril was a stranger to her. I soon discovered she was a positive encyclopedia on plants and, moreover, thoroughly enjoyed her role as teacher.

I asked where she had learned so much about her 'green people'. "From Grandma," she exclaimed. "I help her gathering herbs." What a remarkable child! I am much taken with her, as — it delights me to say — she appears to be with me. And I could not have found a better teacher. Melanie has reawakened in me the love of Nature, the joy of knowledge gained in carefree wanderings out-of-doors which, as a boy, led me to become a scientist.

Arctium longevus

This is a rare species known only to Dinotopia, related to the common burdock genus of the Old and New Worlds. Deep-rooted, and growing to a height of three to six feet, it bears purple flowers with hooked bristles. Tinctures of the flowers are used in medicinal healing, especially to promote strong wing membranes among the pterosaurs.

The root is gathered, dried, and prepared in a tea-like infusion, using waters of the springs near Bent Root, and offered to humans after they have reached twenty-four summers. The claim often made is that the tea changes the body's chemistry to reverse the ageing process. Thus a human can approach or even exceed the long lifespans of the dinosaurs, known to live beyond their 250th year.

I met a small, wrinkled man from Cornucopia who claimed to be Cornelis Huyghen, born in Holland in the year 1618, and to have been one of four crewmen shipwrecked from a Dutch East India vessel. He spoke with such familiarity about the old pepper ports on the coast of Java, and other antiquities that I could not easily discredit his story.

Whether or not the claims are true I cannot say. Nevertheless, as a practical man — and as a scientist interested in making even such a long-term experiment — I now make a habit of drinking the tea of *A. longevus*. This is obviously the "herb" to which Nallab so airily referred back in Waterfall City.

Chenopodium tluca

To Dinotopians, corn and wheat are virtually unknown: instead they cultivate a variety of unfamiliar grains, including a variant of quinoa. The tiny seeds are dried and steamed into a nutty-flavored mash, or ground to flour and converted into delicious pancakes and dumplings.

The Aztecs used the whole plant and all its parts for many different purposes and worshipped it as a source of life. After their subjugation by the Spanish, the sacred grain was kept alive in hidden pockets in the mountains.

In 1582, a crewman named Tluca Uman of Aztec descent was traveling aboard the *San Pedro*. When his ship was wrecked, he was rescued by dolphins, along with his cache of *C. tluca* seeds, safely sealed in coconut shells. The plant has flourished on Dinotopia ever since.

Tluca Uman's likeness, in full headdress, and astride a dolphin, is often seen painted on dinnerware — an appropriate place for a symbol of plenty.

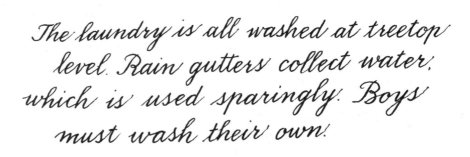

Ladder to the
Beehives
↓

The laundry is all washed at treetop
level. Rain gutters collect water,
which is used sparingly. Boys
must wash their own.

Will's experience in the rigging while at sea has made him right at home at these heights.

Everyone wants me to try this swing.

The Brachiosaurus encourages some dangerous stunts. Fortunately there is a leaf pile underneath.

Bix likes to get into long musical conversations with prosauropods

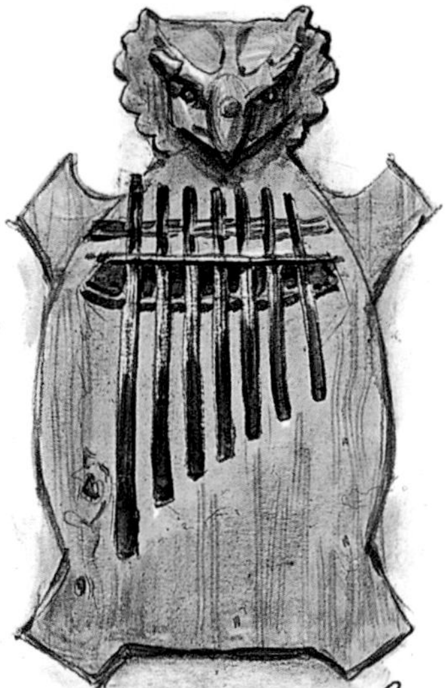

The sauropod dinosaurs use musical notes to communicate with each other and with humans. Like whales or dolphins, they begin with an upward glide as a "search" call. A downward glide indicates concern or distress. A rapidly rising and falling series suggests great excitement or irritation. From these simple beginnings, a rich musical language has developed.

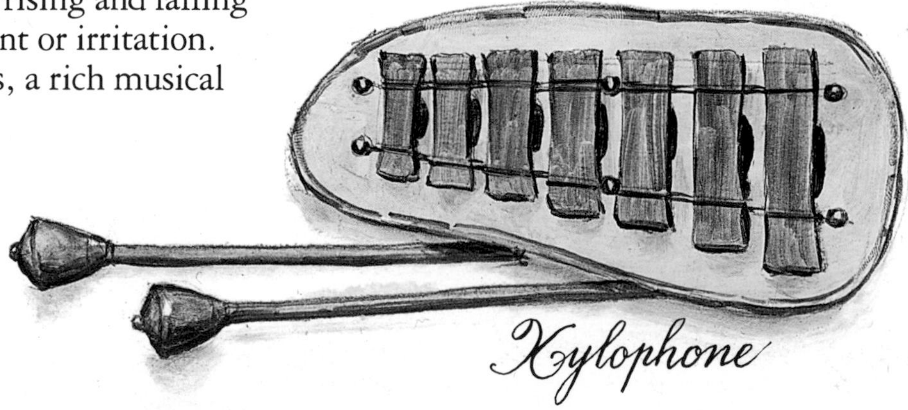

Bamboo Panpipes

Thumb Piano

Xylophone

"Rising sun."

"Rainfall"

"Water flowing underground"

'Pose dancing' is a vocabulary of gestures performed by a human / dinosaur pair.

Ordinary human vision

We have spent many weeks living with and studying the habits of dinosaurs. Soon this training period will come to an end, but Bix has particularly asked me to make these pictures to show how dinosaurs see. The world through her eyes is evidently different from what we see.

Dinosaur eyes take in a wider field of view, bending in at the edges like a glass globe filled with water. Nothing is gray or drab or dull; rather they see swimming particles of color, a moving mosaic of dancing colored specks. As we would see a starscape in the night sky, they see a sparkling "lifescape" in the woods by day, a world teeming with life.

Some humans can see with dinosaur vision, Bix explained: artists, poets, and children. But for the rest of us, as we grow older, the mammalian part of the brain clouds over the older reptilian part, and drains away a little of the glory of the world.

Dinosaur vision

A Song of Dinotopia

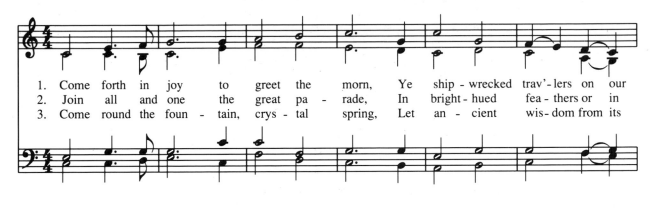

1. Come forth in joy to greet the morn, Ye ship - wrecked trav'- lers on our
2. Join all and one the great pa - rade, In bright - hued fea - thers or in
3. Come round the foun - tain, crys - tal spring, Let an - cient wis - dom from its

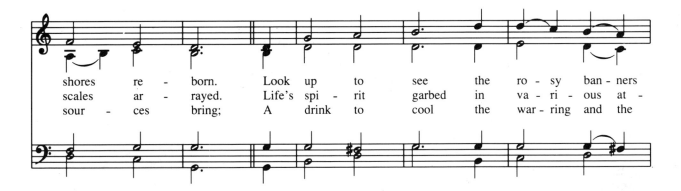

shores re - born. Look up to see the ro - sy ban - ners
scales ar - rayed. Life's spi - rit garbed in va - ri - ous at -
sour - ces bring; A drink to cool the war - ring and the

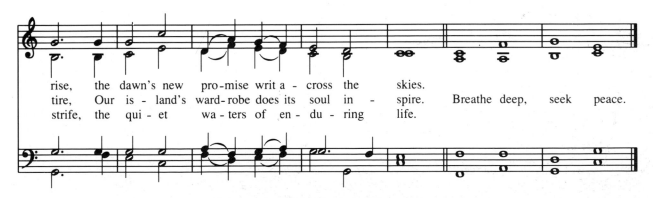

rise, the dawn's new pro - mise writ a - cross the skies.
tire, Our is - land's ward - robe does its soul in - spire. Breathe deep, seek peace.
strife, the qui - et wa - ters of en - du - ring life.

4. Take up the chisel and the drum!
   Each adding flourishes with claw or thumb;
   So glorious cities rise from stony ground,
   Advancing skyward with triumphal sound.

Stegosaurus is a most fastidious animal.

Camarasaurus needs dental work often.

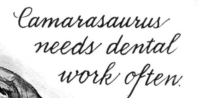

When around strangers Styracosaurus needs to be re-assured with a rub under the chin

"Skyhopping" is a popular sport.

At the end of the training season, the young people take part in the Dinosaur Olympics, the crowning contest of which is the Ring Riding Event, held each year in Cornucopia, a settlement near Treetown.

Northwest Northeast Southwest Southeast

A legendary saddle from the 1650's

The object of the event is to capture the greatest number of rings of the proper color. The banners strung across the track represent each of the four quadrants of the island. Rings are loosely attached with strips of paper.

The saddle holds two riders: a young woman in front, who steers by touch signals, and a young man standing in back, who catches the rings on a pole as he races past. Together with the skill and instinct of their steed, the *Deinocheirus*, they make a trio.

The human riders are selected by Norah. To Will's keen pleasure, he was paired with Sylvia, the two of them representing the Hatchery Sector of the entire Northwest quadrant. Sylvia's rapport with dinosaurs is going to be extremely important.

To understand the singular nature of the *Deinocheirus*, imagine an ostrich growing three times its ordinary height, climbing into the skin of an elephant, diving into a river of bright-hued paint, and then prancing about with the arrogance of a camel. Will, Sylvia, and the other contestants spent days practicing with their temperamental mounts.

Race Day saw crowds pouring into the rustic stadium from all the villages around Deep Lake, leaving not a single child in his dooryard, not a single velvet robe in its closet, not a single hat on its peg.

After many hours of feasting and dancing, a lone trumpet call from the edge of the forest brought all to silent attention. Then of a sudden the crash of a cymbal woke the multitude into a frenzy of excitement. A small *Dimorphodon*, flying ahead to set the pace, careened around the great ring, just ahead of the feet of the running giants. At first I tried to sketch, but I found myself yelling encouragement and leaping up and down along with the screaming spectators.

Will and Sylvia rounded the track, once, twice, three times: sometimes missing a ring with the pole, sometimes catching it, until, before the cymbal was struck again to conclude the running, they had in their possession no less than four of the hard-won rings, the most of any team.

My son's team was triumphant! Many hands slapped my shoulder in congratulation; many long-necked dinosaurs swung their heads toward me in a gesture of approbation. Although I had done nothing, in fact, to contribute to the victory, I was enveloped in a cloud of happy celebration.

The Ring Riders

Will, Sylvia, and Claw paraded through the crowds, trailing a throng of children. The victorious trio paused to receive the blessing of all the dinosaur elders, many of whom had been present at the meeting months before in the Temple Ruins.

Brokehorn gave each of them a token of good fortune for the journey ahead, and said — this time with Bix translating — "You humans have now cracked through your shell. You are ready to become a Habitat Partner. The earth, the sky, and the sea are all open to you. What region, what zone of life do each of you choose?"

"The sky," was their simultaneous reply.

Will and Sylvia riding "Claw," a Deinocheirus

This triumph means they are assured of going on to Canyon City to train as Skybax Riders.

We soon departed for Canyon City. I was sorry to go away and leave Norah and Melanie, even for the mysteries that surely lay ahead to the east, where Will and Sylvia could finish their training. For Will, drawn upward by the eagerness to fly, and for me, drawn forward by the hunger for new discovery, the rootless life offered its own consolation. But I will miss my friends.

We made uncommonly good progress through the Northern Plains, riding upon the high backs of migrating *Apatosauruses*, affording us a fine view of the foothills of the Backbone Mountains.

One morning, after brooding a while in silence, Will turned to Bix and asked, "What did he mean—about Sylvia and I 'just cracking through the shell?' Did he see us as living inside an egg all the time before?"

"You must understand, Will, that Brokehorn sees all human young as protected—that is, as eggs. It was a great compliment. Cracking through the shell is no easy task, nor is living without a yolk sac." Will saw nothing odd in this. He is settling comfortably into human-saurian relationships.

Eventually a strong wind coming off a ridge announced our approach to Canyon City. We disembarked at the edge, seeing before us, yawning and beckoning, a dreamland of air and stone.

To a man who cannot fly, Canyon City, and its nearby Skybax rookery, known as Pteros, is like a wharf to a man without a boat. I had hoped to find Skybaxes lined up like gondolas in Venice, with dashing tour guides ready to take me aloft. But only one rider can fit at a time on the special saddle, and that rider must know his mount better than a falconer knows his bird.

But to the earthbound traveler many wonders are within the scope of a network of trails and bridges. I have just returned, for instance, from a fine concert by a single *Edmontosaurus*, who used the echo effect of a natural amphitheater to produce sustained notes of a chord, punctuated by rhythmic bark-coughs.

Many of the apartments are carved into solid rock, or built up from brick and nestled under rocky ledges. The windows are small, covered with paper rather than glass. The inside walls of the human dwellings are painted with frescoes of frolicking dolphins and bright wildflowers in a Minoan style.

The villagers grow cotton, peppers, and squash on narrow ledges above the canyon, which drops down, layer by layer, to the bottom, 145 necks (5800 feet) in vertical distance. The Amu River, if visible at all, appears a mere twisted brown thread. As the changing afternoon sun brings new areas into bold relief, I fancy I see vast shapes in the rocky walls. I must find a way to investigate.

Each morning before dawn, Will crawls out of his bed (in a niche in the wall) and takes the two-hour climb to the Skybax rookery. Like many of the dinosaur abodes I have seen, the rookery has none of the square corners and flat geometry of our European architecture, blending instead with the natural flowing forms in the rock, and decorated with designs of interlocking circles or spirals.

I will accompany Will tomorrow to watch Oolu, the head instructor, prepare the batch of new pilots.

Wall fresco, Canyon City

Oolu, Skybax instructor

Oolu and the student fliers assembled on a ledge beneath the glowing canopy of the Skybax's wings. The creature preened and stretched, shuffled and ambled, folding and refolding its wings, and finally perched awkwardly.

"Please keep in mind that this is a pterosaur, not a dinosaur," said Oolu. "It will not understand your human or saurian languages.

"In ancient days, the two large pterosaurs, *Pteranodon* and *Quetzalcoatlus skybax* parted ways. The Skybax took to the heights above the earth, and chose the rainbow as its sign. The *Pteranodon* remained in the canyons as gatekeeper to the World Beneath. Both have a needed role to play in the canyons, but you must honor the fact that they are old brothers who have their differences.

"You will discover," continued Oolu, "that your Skybax will not fly beyond the Sentinels, who guard the lower canyon. That boundary cannot be crossed while you are in flight."

Master pilot

Apprentice

Beginner

[123]

In the coming days, as Will and his fellow fliers began short excursions down the canyon, he discovered the truth of Oolu's words. At the stone Sentinels, each Skybax would wheel around, like a Baltimore Clipper coming about, and return to its accustomed space.

What was the secret business of the canyon? Oolu spoke of the "World Beneath" as if it were an actual place. Could there be any substance to those old charts from Waterfall City? I now felt intensely curious about this mystery.

During all our travels in Dinotopia, we had found the people to be straightforward and genial, encouraging of honest inquiry, hiding no secrets, fearing no taboos. Yet direct questions about the Sentinels now brought an uneasy shrug or, at best, a remark that the region belonged to others. And for once, Bix was of no help. She evaded discreet questions. It seemed I would have to find out for myself.

A Skybax will
not fly beyond
the Sentinels

Oolu had warned only against *flying* beyond the Sentinels. Had anyone explored the region on foot? Yes, indeed, but so long ago that no one really remembered. People, it seemed, did not like to violate the taboo out of respect for the saurians. Would there be any objection to my taking a look in the name of science? No, indeed — but their tone was doubtful. If I chose to go, that was my decision to make.

Will and I spoke long into the night about this exploration. To my amusement, he disapproved of my "poking about." But he agreed to come part way, at least to the bottom of the canyon, despite Sylvia's strong-minded opposition.

We provisioned for the expedition: dry food, light blanket, oil-wrapped notepaper. Although Will had offered to keep the Journal up to date, of course I would also need to make my own notes below. I wore my old coat and reinforced my footwear, envisioning a fairly rough journey.

We descended the cliffs by an old trail that was still in use. It stopped at the water's edge, and we were obliged to wade or scramble as we proceeded south. We reached the confluence of the Ancient Gorge some ten miles below Canyon City and made camp. Here tumbling green and white waters mingled with the brown of the Amu. By firelight the rocky walls above the water showed a distinct sheen, not of natural erosion, but as if something had rubbed them to a polished surface.

The next day we followed the pathway of the rubbed walls beyond the point of the Sentinels, where, rounding a turn of the river, we came upon an extraordinary sight: strange monuments, Egyptian in character, along with carvings that suggested the first meetings between humans and dinosaurs. Fascinated, we were drawn on.

We swam through a sunken canyon of old monuments

The historical reliefs

We continued further downstream.
Even before we saw the *Pteranodons*, we
expected them. The smell of death hung
heavy in the air. The bodies of dead dinosaurs
lay about us, being scoured to the bone by the
scavengers. The *Pteranodons* did not attack us, but
flew up, alarmed and aggravated, to the top of an isolated
bluff, where they followed our progress with sober interest.

Portal to the World Beneath

There was no horror for us in this landscape of decay. It was hushed and somber, clearly a holy place to the great creatures, who in their last days would come here by choice to review the sacred sculptures and to give their flesh for the renewal of life.

A deep rumble ahead drew us forward to find a vast circular opening into which the waters of the Amu River plunged. A broad spiral pathway, carved from the rock by ancient claws, led downward from the brink. But at this point Will thought he should go no further.

"Wait here, Will," I said. "I'm going down to have a look ahead." I descended the sloping ledge some 100 feet to find the river had created a deep channel into the earth, surmounted by vaulted rock and flanked by a safe walkway. A blast of fresh, scented air cooled my face. I pushed forward. Now I could see a strange illumination, a phosphorescence, that shone upon growing plants: mosses, ferns, and

then shrubs growing in wild profusion. Among them was *Taraxacum officinale*, which I knew to be edible. I surmised that I lacked nothing to sustain me on a much longer journey.

I scrambled back to the surface to find Will looking upward. High above, in the small patch of sky that remained visible above the surrounding curtains of stone, his Skybax was descending, showing concern for Will by daring to enter the hallowed territory of the *Pteranodon*.

"This is the chance of a lifetime for me," I said to Will, "the doorway to a whole new world." I reassured him that I had ample provisions and would return in a few weeks, and thanked him again for undertaking to keep the Journals, despite the new demands on his time. I am poor at expressing the pride I feel in my boy. "Good luck with your training," I said, as we parted.

I watched him swoop upward with a rush of wings. Then I turned to descend into the earth.

The busy weeks have passed. As I write for the first time in this book, I can almost feel my father beside me.

Our training is hard. Lying in the saddle makes my shoulders and neck really hurt. Cirrus has a fierce independence, and she will not be controlled. After seeing her to her roost, I often spend the evenings with Sylvia and Bix, sometimes at Bix's home. "Sylvia won't be controlled, either," says Bix. I don't know what she means. I am not *trying* to control Sylvia — only Cirrus. Anyway, no one could control Sylvia. Look how she talked to my father when he went off. I wonder where he is now.

Bix says the caves are part of a huge network. No one goes down there now, but it once sheltered all island life. Bix says that somewhere in the canyon walls the story is carved: long, long ago, before humans started coming, the sky went black with dust and it got very cold. The dinosaurs collected seeds, spores, insects — everything — and took themselves and the whole lot underground. Something like Noah's Ark. Later, when the air got clear again, everything came back to the surface. The same ramp that my father went down was the one the dinosaurs used to come out. Dinosaurs travel past the Sentinels to die because it feels like coming home.

It's been a month since father left. How could it be a month? I feel I understand Cirrus better. She now lets me treat her wings with burdock medicine. Yesterday we practiced launching and landing in a strong headwind. Besides flying there's a whole lot of study about clouds and winds. At least I'm better at study than Sylvia. Bix says it's my father coming out in me. He ought to be back soon. Oolu has been working with me to change the habits I learned with horses. Stop *steering*, he yells. Sylvia is lucky; she

Skylight

Shell lamp

family visits last many days.

Home of Bix, with her elder nestmate Hylo and mother Petra.

Speaking platform

never learned bad habits. I asked Oolu again today when we might be considered for full apprenticeship.

"Cirrus and Nimbus will tell you when you're ready," he said. "You need to win *their* respect. You cannot ask them to carry you aloft until you have a feel for what it takes to climb up through the air with a heavy weight on your back. You have to show them you are not tied to the earth."

"How can I do that?" I said. "I can't fly."

"You can climb," he said. "You've got feet, and you can carry a backpack." He pointed toward the mountains with his chin. "Up there, at the top you'll find an old building called the Tentpole of the Sky. Other Riders have made the climb, but you would be the first Dolphinback. Sylvia should climb beside you; you might need her help. It's a hard trip, but think of Cirrus and Nimbus; you'll win full partners from it."

Bix blinked when we invited her along. "No, no, not for me," she said. "This is for you. I am no mountain climber, and besides, I have some family business to attend to."

[133]

Some weeks later, Sylvia and I left Canyon City, saying goodbye to our human and saurian friends. Oolu assured us my father would return, that he would somehow be taken care of. Cirrus and Nimbus waited for us at the trail head. It was hard to leave them, especially when Cirrus folded me in her wings. Then as Sylvia and I left, they both stretched out their wings in a slow flap, like waving goodbye. Sylvia was crying. I couldn't put my arm around her because of the backpacks, but I held her hand.

As far as the eastern foothills of the Forbidden Mountains the way was easy. Sometimes we met an occasional traveler. Even this far from the sea there were monuments — the work of dinosaurs, Sylvia says — raised to honor sea creatures such as trilobites, nautiloids, or sea scorpions.

A monument to trilobites

"Cirrus"

[134]

Moropus, Brontotherium,
ancient mammals
who live in the mountains

In a few days the wide dinosaur roads thinned out, replaced by footpaths leading up along the streams. We began to climb through thickly wooded valleys of silver fir, giving way to dwarf rhododendron. Sylvia found minty groundcreepers, which she collected to brew into a fine tea. For some days we had a bad time, slowed by giant piles of sharp boulders, some larger than a house, scattered around, sometimes separated by foaming torrents. I was worried, too, about sabertooths, so I found a stout, sharp pole. Sylvia laughed. I didn't mind — the pole came in handy for climbing. From the high, barren places, we were able to look down on the Canyon: it looked like a small scratch in a table. Once we thought we saw Cirrus and Nimbus far off, watching us. But it might have been other Skybaxes.

We reached our first goal, a village shared by humans and large mammals: giant ground sloths, glyptodonts, and camels, by nature more restless and rugged than dinosaurs.

A fine sympathetic mammoth, a cousin of Bigtusk, offered to carry us as far as he could, being familiar with the terrain. He had good footing, even on ice, and he found overhangs for us each night, sealing our shelters with the warmth of his great body. After even he had to turn back, we scaled the mountain on foot. With each ridge we climbed, the remote building far above us seemed to float up higher, disappearing from time to time in mist. By turn we encouraged each other, Sylvia never complaining, and during the freezing nights we huddled together.

'Tentpole of the Sky'

At last, at the end of a very long day, we reached the summit, resting our backpacks thankfully against the foundation stones. The clouds thickened, snuffing out the final flickers of sunlight. Above us, bells rang out (we later learned they announced the "raising of the black tent," that is, the onset of night). We shouted for many minutes, until, to our great relief, first one face and then several leaned out over the parapet. A rope ladder dropped to the snow beside me.

After being greeted, we were led straight to our host, Levka Gambo, who lost no time in refreshing us with hot buttered tea in clay cups, blankets of woven fur (the first we had seen in Dinotopia), and a strong aromatic incense. All this combined to lull us into an exhausted, dreamless sleep.

Next morning, after a simple breakfast, we toured the old frescoes and learned some history. Far as we were from dinosaurs, we felt their good will, for this magnificent building was their idea — although built by Tibetans. The dinosaurs realized that certain newcomers benefited from being isolated. Some people needed to be private for a time, removed from reminders of all they had lost, until they were ready to take on a new life. Nothing could be more removed than this place. Since no trails can be maintained, supplies are brought in by a floating balloon-boat called a Sky Galley.

The Map Room

Living at the top of the mountain has begun to cast a curious spell over me. At dawn the silence is utter and absolute. From the balconies on clear mornings, I can trace the course of both great rivers, the Amu and the Polongo. I can even see a tiny grain of white that must be

Waterfall City. Late at night, or when the wind is howling about the cold stones outside, I sometimes venture down to the Map Room, housed in the belly of the building. To my great delight, I have found a chart showing the extensive caves of the World Beneath. Apparently there are

Levka Gambo

many luminous passages and chambers, and several portals through which my father might exit — although, knowing him, I realize he would not stop until he satisfies his curiosity. I told Levka about his journey, and he seemed to sense the turn of my thoughts.

"You will find your father again," he said, "but neither of you will be the same." I pressed him to explain. "Each person who arrives in Dinotopia becomes reborn, and the birth is different for each individual. Your father will be born of the Earth. You and Sylvia will be born of the Sky."

SYLVIA AGREED WITH ME that Levka is a very ancient man. I hesitated to ask his age but she teased me until I did, whereupon he said, "I have long given up measuring the years —" and, eyes twinkling, added, "as I told your young friend!"

Sylvia's mischievous gaiety has reached out to the other keepers of the Tentpole. I have often listened to their laughter as she studies the intricately beautiful weaving they do, using fur shed by mammals. Both of us help with chores. Even though we're together most of the time, she often seems lost in her own thoughts. She's still a mystery to me.

A great deal has happened since writing the above. One morning our routine was interrupted by Levka, who sat us down and handed each of us a stack of very old, faded picture-cards. "Look through these," he said. "Choose just one to return to me." Absorbed, I considered each image: a bridge, a house, a fish, a flame, a moon, a cloud, a flower, and a trilobite. I put the cloud card into his waiting hand just as Sylvia gave him hers. Our eyes met. Levka held up the cards — twin clouds. We both knew at once that this was a turning point. Levka had known, too, and earlier must have sensed the Sky Galley approaching from afar, for there it was, drifting on the horizon. By the time we'd packed and said goodbye, it was looming over-head, secured by its drag line to a bronze ring.

As winches lowered the bundles of cargo, Levka turned to us and smiled. "Breathe deep," he said. "Fly high. Seek peace." Then he gestured us up the ladder. We followed the galley-man and crouched in the boat-like gondola. The rope was freed, and we watched in silence as the snowy peaks dropped away.

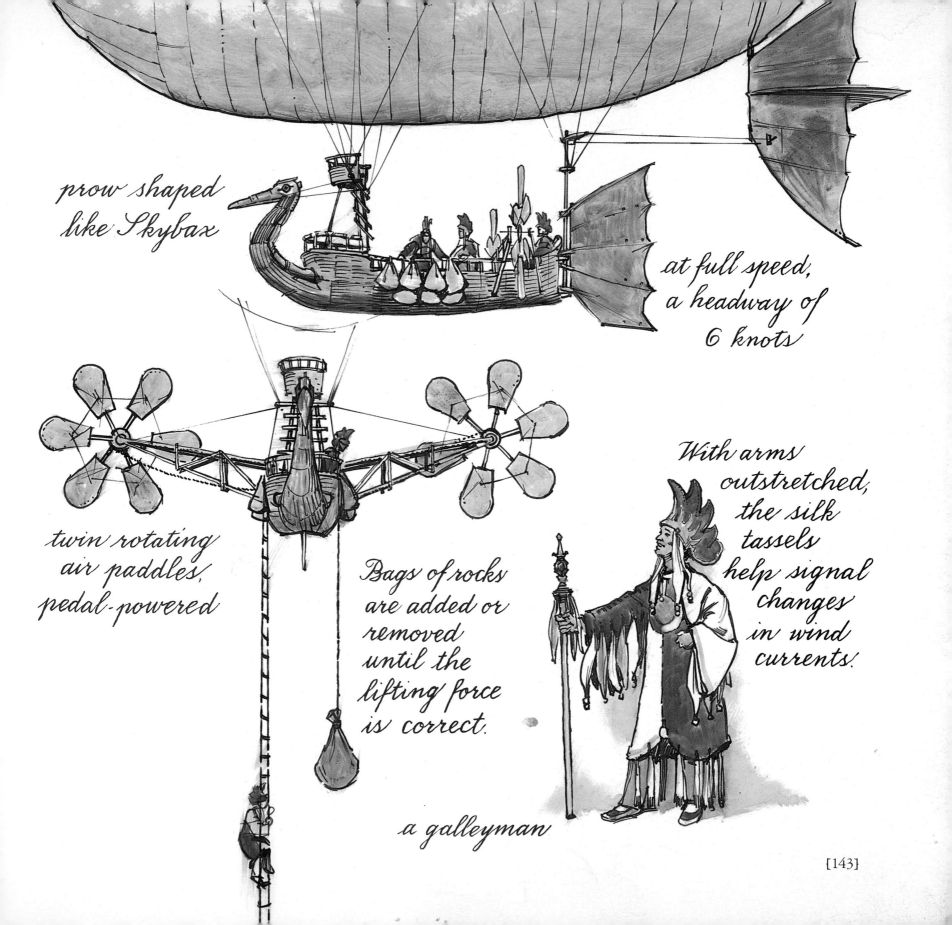

prow shaped like *Skybax*

at full speed, a headway of 6 knots

twin rotating air paddles, pedal-powered

Bags of rocks are added or removed until the lifting force is correct.

a galleyman

With arms outstretched, the silk tassels help signal changes in wind currents.

At first we drifted like a leaf on a lazy river, revolving slowly as the sun alternately warmed each side of the gas envelope. Until we began to pedal, all was silent and serene. Pairs of galleymen took turns at the squeaky pedals, which moved us along fast enough to feel the bitter air on our faces.

The galleymen knew Canyon City well — one was a retired Skybax Rider — and were pleased to carry us as far east as they could. But the sea of clouds under us was beginning to look ruffled and uncertain. By the fourth hour, we struck a hot updraft from the eastern face of the Forbidden Mountains, and we noticed the world sinking even further away. The sky above was a dark, deep blue, the air so thin we were panting. A tug on a red rope released precious helium, and we reversed direction, plunging down into the clouds. We dropped perilously low, despite bag after bag being cut free. Violent gusts hurled us about, plunging us at one moment into gray obscurity, and the next desperately near the rocky clutches of the mountains. It was a solemn kind of fury, quite unlike the wild screaming of the typhoon that wrecked our ship. When we stopped pedaling, the only sound was the soft groaning of the gondola and the eerie whistling of the wind over the mountain passes.

Poor Sylvia was in misery from the swinging and spinning. I held her securely in my arms and soothed her, telling her that whatever happened, we would be together. In the fading light we could see that the ropework and the rudder had been damaged. The galleymen jettisoned everything they could, but still the balloon scarcely held us aloft.

At some point each of us realized we had lost all control. There was nothing left to do. Darkness overcame us, but oddly enough, I felt no fear. We all wrapped up in as much covering as possible and secured ourselves for a hard landing.

But our aimless flight took many more hours. There was no sense of movement or direction. Sylvia and I even dozed off for a time, and woke to the feel of warmer air.

Suddenly a galleyman shouted, but his words were lost in several bouncing jolts that ended in a splintering crash. Luckily the final impact was softened by what later turned out to be a field of flowers. At the time, after making sure no one was seriously hurt, we all curled up on the ground and slept, exhausted, until dawn woke us to reveal a shattered ship.

In the growing light we could see a large city on the horizon. Our pilots recognized it instantly — Sauropolis, capital of Dinotopia. After eating what remained of our food, we set out.

Even from a distance away, through the grand entrance gate we could hear music and laughter. Apparently no one had been able to observe our crash. We simply joined the stream of people — all carrying flowers and colored banners — and entered the capital city.

A crowd of merrymakers
preparing for a parade
swept us up in its
spirit of happy abandon.

Sylvia took my arm and we drifted like dragon-flies, careless of the sudden rattle of drumbeats, the blare of trumpets, or the squeals of children running wildly past us, their long-tailed nannies in anxious pursuit. I know there was some residue left in me from the solitary mountaintop peace, and the sky-tossed surrender that we had just experienced. Sylvia moved beside me, and I felt great joy knowing she had shared in every step of the journey. My father had once told me the words of Malik, the timekeeper: " — the whole earth has a heartbeat." Now for the first time, I sensed that pulse of life animating all of us, every creature, large and small.

Presently a woman, apparently an official of the city, approached us, looked us up and down, and exclaimed, "It's you! Sylvia and Will."

"Yes, you're right," said Sylvia, puzzled that we would be recognized.

"Great eruptions! Did you know — ? Of course not. Arthur and Bix have arrived. That is, they've left. Oh, you've just missed them. They left for Waterfall City a few days ago. It's a three day trip by land, so they should — "

"My father and Bix?" I interrupted. "What were they doing *here*? They should have been in Canyon City."

"Well, I don't know about that. They were certainly here. They arrived by sea, popping up right in the harbor, in a most extraordinary vessel. Come, I'll show you."

Bewildered, we followed our guide to the harbor. An odd and primitive craft was hoisted up on display. Glass domes, brass hatches, coils, straps, hinges, and steering fins fitted roughly together in what appeared to be an underwater vessel.

"Isn't it ingenious?" said the woman. "Put together by Arthur, with the help of Bix."

I was amazed. I had no idea my father was so handy with machines.

"My father must have found a way out of the World Beneath," I said. Sylvia excitedly agreed. The woman suggested we immediately send a message by signal tower to Oolu to request our Skybaxes, and permission to fly them. A fanfare sounded in the distance.

"While you're waiting for your Skybaxes," the woman said, "do join our parade. How lucky that you arrived today — it is our festival to honor children and hatchlings."

The submersible vessel

Rudder

Breathing pipes, with valves

Propeller for ascent

Balance chamber and depth gauge

Stabilizing fin

Bottom skid

Propeller for motion forward or astern, hand-cranked

SAUROPOLIS

Rather than joining the parade, Sylvia and I were content just to watch, to see the spectacle unfold as if in a dream. Sylvia was given a basket of violets and a tiara of daisies. I will see her so forever in my mind, whatever happens in the future. I was not really certain of her feelings, although sure of my own. One thing I realized — our parents would think us both too young for *cumspiritik*. But at least we are going to share the life of Skybax Rider together.

At last, Cirrus and Nimbus arrived, to our great joy. Strapped to their saddles were our new flying outfits, emblazoned on the shoulders with the badge of Apprentice. We unrolled a note from Oolu: "Congratulations! You don't need my permission: you have theirs. Fly high, seek peace."

Cirrus and Nimbus carried us to the landing platform of Waterfall City. We stood for a moment, thrilled to feel again the cascading thunder of the waters. Before long Bix arrived, wiggling with excitement.

Sylvia knelt down. "Why didn't you tell us you were going in after Arthur?"

"I didn't want to make you worry. You had your own work to do. I felt Arthur might be in need of some assistance."

"But for a dinosaur — going to the World Beneath — wasn't that breaking an old custom?" I said.

"We Ambassadors have freedom to go wherever we can be of service. Now come, there's someone who wants to see you."

She took us to the library, where at last we found
my father, the center of an eager throng of geogra-
phers and historians. He broke off as soon as he saw
me to rush over and hug me for the first time since I
was a little boy. When I got my breath back, I said,
"I'm told you just arrived. What happened down
there? Were you in danger?"

"Well, uh —," my father hesitated, "in a way, my
boy, in a way. But — Oh, Will, you won't believe
the wonders I've seen, the fantastic discoveries —"
he put his arm around Sylvia, "but the truth is, I
have never — never in all my life — been so glad to
see any two people!"

the new
studio,
with easy access
to the library —
and to the falls!

Reunited, we stood
and watched
the falls.

Journal of Arthur Denison

I HAVE READ WILL'S NOTES, and I smile at the transformation they reveal. When I left him he was a boy. He entered the library door a young man. Seeing Will and Sylvia both wearing the uniform of the Skybax Rider fills me with a father's pride. Will has the furrowed brow and the square shoulders of a man of purpose. And from the little glances they exchange, Will and Sylvia have become good friends who respect — and love — each other.

Have I changed as well? Perhaps so. My friends from the dear old world we left so long ago on the wharf in Boston — those fellows surely would wag their heads at me. But I wonder if I shall ever see their faces again. No matter. Our old life was richly rewarding, and I am grateful to it. But here on Dinotopia my eyes have been opened to the wonders of a new world. Seeing with fresh eyes has rejuvenated me. I find enormous enthusiasm filling my mind. Nallab has given me a simple studio overlooking the falls, a home for my spiral pocket watch, my plumes and pencils, my maps, my designs — and most of all my recent field notes, which at the moment are in disarray, having been made under difficult circumstances in the World Beneath. There is a lifetime — a long lifetime — of work to do here. I cannot start soon enough.